www.randomhouse.com/kids

Educators and librarians, for a variety of teaching tools, visit us at www.randomhouse.com/teachers

Library of Congress Cataloging-in-Publication Data
Freeman, Martha, 1956–
Mrs. Wow never wanted a cow / by Martha Freeman ; illustrated by Steven Salerno. — 1st ed.
p. cm.
"Beginner books." SUMMARY: When Mrs. Wow takes in a stray cow, her lazy dog and cat hope to train
the new household member to catch mice and intimidate the mailman.
ISBN 0-375-83418-4 (trade) — ISBN 0-375-93418-9 (lib. bdg.) — ISBN 0-375-83419-2 (board)
[1. Cows—Fiction. 2. Dogs—Fiction. 3. Cats—Fiction.] I. Salerno, Steven, ill. II. Title.
PZ7.F87496Mrs 2006
[E]—dc22
2005006000

Printed in the United States of America
First Edition   15

Mrs. Wow Never Wanted a Cow

By Martha Freeman · Illustrated by Steven Salerno

BEGINNER BOOKS®

A Division of Random House, Inc.

One day, Mrs. Wow was
out mowing her grass.
There stood a cow.

Mrs. Wow tried to shoo the cow.
But the cow did not shoo.

Mrs. Wow never wanted
a cow!

Mrs. Wow had a cat
named Meow.

Meow's chore was
to catch mice.

But she loved
to sleep.

Mrs. Wow also had a
lazy dog named Bow-Wow.

Bow-Wow's chore was to guard the house.

But he loved
to eat.

When Meow and Bow-Wow
saw the big, strong cow,
they got an idea.
They would show her how
to do their chores.
Then they could sleep and eat
all day!

Meow and Bow-Wow begged
Mrs. Wow to let the cow stay.
Mrs. Wow never wanted a cow.
But she loved her
lazy, crazy pets.

"We will keep
the cow," she said,
"for now."

Meow showed the cow
how to catch a mouse.
She swished her tail.
She wiggled her rump.
Then . . .

. . . pounce!

She got the mouse.

Now it was the cow's turn.

The cow swished her tail.

The cow did not wiggle her rump.

The cow walked up to the mouse

and . . .

. . . zip!
The mouse ran away.

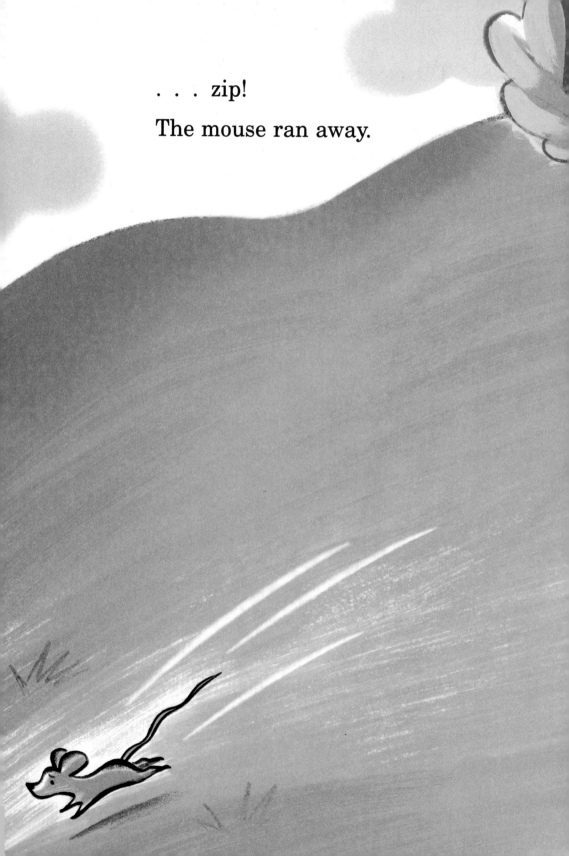

Meow shook her head.
"The cow is useless!"
she said.

When the mailman came,
Bow-Wow showed the cow how
to guard the house.
He bared his teeth.

He growled.

GRRRRRRRRR

He barked. . . .

"Rowf-rowf-rowf!"
The mailman hid
behind a bush.
Now it was the cow's turn.

The cow blinked her eyes.

The cow chewed some grass.

The cow said, "Moo-oo-oo."

The mailman did not hide.
He gave the cow a friendly
pat on the rump.

Bow-Wow shook his head.

"The cow is useless!" he said.

Mrs. Wow stopped mowing
the grass.
"What is the matter?" she asked.

Meow told Mrs. Wow
about the mouse.
Bow-Wow told Mrs. Wow
about the mailman.

"The cow is useless!"
they said.
"We will have to do
our own chores!"

Mrs. Wow laughed
at her lazy, crazy pets.
"Don't you know a cow
can only do two things?"
said Mrs. Wow.
"Cows eat grass,
and cows give milk."

Mrs. Wow got an idea.
"This cow **is** useful!"
she said.
She gave the cow
a friendly pat
on the rump.

Now Mrs. Wow has
two new chores.
She milks the cow.